This book belongs to

....

The Autumn Princess

Nick and Claire Page

Illustrations by Beverley Young

make
believe
ideas

The Autumn Princess had damson-red hair and eyes the colour of greengages. She helped her parents, the King and Queen of Autumn, to look after everything in the Old Orchard.

She loved talking to the apple trees in
the orchard. They had names like Bess Pool,
Black Jack, Annie Elizabeth, Crimson Costard,
Cornish Gillyflower and Gipsy King.

Her favourite was Golden Pippin. He let her climb his branches and gave her delicious fruit. When the wind blew, he would rock her to sleep. The other trees could talk, but Golden Pippin was silent and a little sad.

One day, the king and queen said, "It is time for us to look after another orchard. You must take over here. We shall find someone to look after you and help you."

The king said, "You need someone down-to-earth, to keep you safe from harm."

The queen said, "No, you need someone to lift you up, to show you new adventures."

So Old Oak, the wisest and oldest tree in the orchard, announced a contest: "Whoever loves the princess the most shall marry her!"

Immediately, the Prince of the Earth
burst from underground! He was dressed
in a blue-black suit of softest velvet.
"Autumn Princess," he said, "I have loved
you from the depths of the earth. We
will be happy and safe underground."

"Super!" said the king. "That's settled then."

But the Autumn Princess said,
"I can't live under the ground. I need the orchard and the orchard needs me. But thank you for your offer."

Then the Prince of the Air came down from the sky! He was dressed in a blue-black coat of finest feathers. "Autumn Princess," he said, "I have loved you from the heights of the sky. We will be happy and free in the clouds."

"Super!" said the queen. "That decides it."
But the Autumn Princess said, "I can't
live up in the sky. I need the orchard
and the orchard needs me. But thank
you for applying."

"The Prince of the Earth has won!" said the king.
"The Prince of the Air has won!" said the queen.
"But I don't want either of them!" said the Autumn Princess.
And she burst into tears and ran off.

She sat at the foot of Golden Pippin
and wept. The tree drank in her tears
as they fell. He showered her with a
blanket of leaves and dropped two
apples, like tears, for her to eat.

Old Oak saw this and said, "I know who truly loves the Autumn Princess. He is rooted in the ground but he reaches into the sky. He can keep her safe and allow her to climb."

"**Super**," said the king and the queen. **"Who?"**
"Golden Pippin," said Old Oak.
"She can't marry a tree!" said the king.
"You'll have to trust me on this one,"
replied Old Oak.

They said to the princess, **"We know who loves you the most."**

"Who?" she asked.

"Golden Pippin," they said.

The princess burst into tears, but this time because she was so happy.

They said to Golden Pippin,
**"Will you look after the
Autumn Princess?"**

"He can't speak," said the princess.
"Just wave your branches, then,"
said the king.

But from deep inside the tree came
the words: "I will."

There was a huge crack! Like a seed breaking open, or a cloud parting to show the sun, the tree opened and out came a handsome prince.

"The enchantment is broken!" boomed Old
Oak. He told how, long ago, a prince had
tried to chop down the orchard. So the magic
of the woods had turned him into a tree,
until he could learn to love the orchard.

Golden Pippin and the Autumn Princess
were married at Apple Harvest. For the rest
of their life together, they looked after the
orchard as no one else ever had or ever will.

Ready to tell

Oh no! Some of the pictures from this story have been mixed up! Can you retell the story and point to each picture in the correct order?

Picture dictionary

Encourage your child to read these harder words from the story and gradually develop their basic vocabulary.

autumn

crack

handsome

harvest

king

orchard

prince

princess

queen

Key words

Here are some key words used in context. Help your child to use other words from the border in simple sentences.

She is **going** away.

Old Oak **was** wise.

Who loves **the** princess?

This tree loves her.

He and **she** are happy.

Host an apple-tasting!

There are many different types of apple. Some traditional varieties have interesting names and may be quite rare.

You will need

5 or 6 eating apples of different types. (It's usually easy to buy Golden Delicious or Pink Lady apples, but can you find less common ones like a Russet or Pippin?) • paper plates (one for each apple) • crayons • green paper • scissors • sticky tape • paper to write on

What to do

1 Colour the paper plates to look like the apples. Cut leaf shapes from the green paper and tape them to the plate.

2 Write a numbered list with the name of each apple.

3 Copy each number onto a different paper plate.

4 Cut each apple into chunks. (Ask a grown-up to help.) Put the pieces on the plate with the matching number.

5 Give each person a piece of paper and a pen or pencil. Ask them to taste each apple and write down what they think about it. For example, do they like its flavour? Is it crunchy or not? Is it sweet or sharp?

6 When everyone has tasted all the apples, get each person to choose his or her favourite.

Now you can tell everyone the name of each apple and enjoy eating them. You could serve apple juice too.